This book belongs to:

_____

For Alan and Amanda – J.W. xx

This paperback edition first published in 2018 by Andersen Press Ltd.
First published in Great Britain in 2017 by Andersen Press Ltd.,
20 Vauxhall Bridge Road, London SW1V 2SA.
Text copyright © Jeanne Willis, 2017.
Illustration copyright © Tony Ross, 2017.
The rights of Jeanne Willis and Tony Ross
to be identified as the author and illustrator of this
work have been asserted by them in accordance with the
Copyright, Designs and Patents Act, 1988.
All rights reserved.
Printed and bound in Malaysia.
1 3 5 7 9 10 8 6 4 2
British Library Cataloguing in Publication Data available.

ISBN 978 1 78344 596 7

The T-Rex who Lost his Specs!

Jeanne Willis

Tony Ross

Ⓐ

ANDERSEN PRESS

There was a T-Rex who lost his specs
and got himself in trouble.

Everything seemed very blurred
and sometimes he saw...

He did not recognise his clothes
when he was getting dressed...

... so put his sister's knickers on
and wore his granny's vest.

He went to give himself a wash
but could not find the basin...

... and so the toilet was the place
that T-Rex washed his face in.

Then when he went to dry himself,
he thought he'd grabbed a towel...

... but rubbed himself all over
with a prehistoric owl.

He went to make his breakfast
but believing they were kippers...

... he fried and ate his brother's sock
and toasted Grandpa's slippers.

And as it was a windy day
he went to fetch his kite.

But as he could not find the string
he tied a new one, tight.

Although the kite put up a fight,
he dragged it through the door,
not realising that it was...

Convinced its cries were just the wind,
the T-Rex climbed the hill...

... in fact a brontosaurus
who was lying very still!

The 'hill' stood up! The 'kite' took off!
What happened to T-Rex?

Some like to think he is extinct
because he lost his specs.

In truth, his best friends saved him but because he could not see,
he thought he had been captured by an evil enemy.

So T-Rex ate them, one by one, and being in a muddle,
he ran to Mum but...

... gave his *real* enemy a cuddle!